Joaquin Miller

Songs of the Mexican seas

Joaquin Miller

Songs of the Mexican seas

ISBN/EAN: 9783743311725

Manufactured in Europe, USA, Canada, Australia, Japa

Cover: Foto ©Andreas Hilbeck / pixelio.de

Manufactured and distributed by brebook publishing software
(www.brebook.com)

Joaquin Miller

Songs of the Mexican seas

SONGS

OF

THE MEXICAN SEAS

BY

JOAQUIN MILLER

AUTHOR OF "SONGS OF THE SIERRAS," "SONGS OF ITALY,"
ETC.

QUI LEGIT REGIT

BOSTON
ROBERTS BROTHERS
1887

TO ABBIE.

Note. — The lines in this little book, as in all my others, were written, or at least conceived, in the lands where the scenes are laid ; so that whatever may be said of the imperfections of my work, I at least have the correct atmosphere and color. I have now and then sent forth from Mexico, and from remoter shores of the Gulf, fragments of these thoughts as they rounded into form, and some of them have been used at a Dartmouth College Commencement, and elsewhere ; but as a whole the book is new.

From the heart of the Sierra, where I once more hear the awful heart-throbs of Nature, I now intrust the first reception of these lessons entirely to my own country. And may I not ask in return, now at the last, when the shadows begin to grow long, something of that consideration which, thus far, has been accorded almost entirely by strangers ?

JOAQUIN MILLER.

MOUNT SHASTA, CALIFORNIA,

    A.D. 1887.

SONGS OF THE MEXICAN SEAS.

THE SEA OF FIRE.

*I*N *that far land, farther than Yucatan,*
  Hondurian height, or Mahogany steep,
Where the great sea, hollowed by the hand of man
  Hears deep come calling across to deep;
Where the great seas follow in the grooves of men
Down under the bastions of Darien:

In that land so far that you wonder whether
  If God would know it should you fall down dead;
In that land so far through the wilds and weather
  That the lost sun sinks like a warrior sped,—
Where the sea and the sky seem closing together,
  Seem closing together as a book that is read:

In that nude warm world, where the unnamed
    rivers
Roll restless in cradles of bright buried gold ;
Where white flashing mountains flow rivers of silver
    As a rock of the desert flowed fountains of old ;
By a dark wooded river that calls to the dawn,
And calls all day with his dolorous swan :

In that land of the wonderful sun and weather,
    With green under foot and with gold over head,
Where the spent sun flames, and you wonder
    whether
    'T is an isle of fire in his foamy bed :
Where the oceans of earth shall be welded together
    By the great French master in his forge flame
    red, —

Lo ! the half-finished world !   Yon footfall re-
    treating, —
It might be the Maker disturbed at his task.
But the footfall of God, or the far pheasant beating,
    It is one and the same, whatever the mask
It may wear unto man.   The woods keep repeating
    The old sacred sermons, whatever you ask.

The brown-muzzled cattle come stealthy to drink,
  The wild forest cattle, with high horns as trim
  As the elk at their side : their sleek necks are slim
And alert like the deer.   They come, then they shrink
  As afraid of their fellows, of shadow-beasts seen
  In the deeps of the dark-wooded waters of green.

It is man in his garden, scarce wakened as yet
  From the sleep that fell on him when woman was
    made.
The new-finished garden is plastic and wet
  From the hand that has fashioned its unpeopled
    shade ;
And the wonder still looks from the fair woman's eyes
As she shines through the wood like the light from
    the skies.

And a ship now and then from some far Ophir's
    shore
  Draws in from the sea.   It lies close to the bank ;
  Then a dull, muffled sound of the slow-shuffled plank
As they load the black ship; but you hear nothing
    more,
  And the dark dewy vines, and the tall sombre wood
  Like twilight droop over the deep sweeping flood.

The black masts are tangled with branches that cross,
The rich, fragrant gums fall from branches to
deck,
The thin ropes are swinging with streamers of moss
That mantle all things like the shreds of a wreck ;
The long mosses swing, there is never a breath :
The river rolls still as the river of death.

I.

IN the beginning, — ay, before
  The six-days' labors were well o'er;
Yea, while the world lay incomplete,
Ere God had opened quite the door
Of this strange land for strong men's feet, —
There lay against that westmost sea
One weird-wild land of mystery.

A far white wall, like fallen moon,
Girt out the world.   The forest lay
So deep you scarcely saw the day,
Save in the high-held middle noon:
It lay a land of sleep and dreams,
And clouds drew through like shoreless streams
That stretch to where no man may say.

Men reached it only from the sea,
By black-built ships, that seemed to creep
Along the shore suspiciously,
Like unnamed monsters of the deep.

It was the weirdest land, I ween,
That mortal eye has ever seen:

A dim, dark land of bird and beast,
Black shaggy beasts with cloven claw, —
A land that scarce knew prayer or priest,
Or law of man, or Nature's law;
Where no fixed line drew sharp dispute
'Twixt savage man and silent brute.

II.

It hath a history most fit
For cunning hand to fashion on;
No chronicler hath mentioned it;
No buccaneer set foot upon.
'T is of an outlawed Spanish Don, —
A cruel man, with pirate's gold
That loaded down his deep ship's hold.

A deep ship's hold of plundered gold!
The golden cruise, the golden cross,
From many a church of Mexico,
From Panama's mad overthrow,

From many a ransomed city's loss,
From many a follower stanch and bold,
And many a foeman stark and cold.

He found this wild, lost land.   He drew
His ship to shore.   His ruthless crew,
Like Romulus, laid lawless hand
On meek brown maidens of the land,
And in their bloody forays bore
Red firebrands along the shore.

III.

The red men rose at night.   They came,
A firm, unflinching wall of flame ;
They swept, as sweeps some fateful sea
O'er land of sand and level shore
That howls in far, fierce agony.
The red men swept that deep, dark shore
As threshers sweep a threshing-floor.

And yet beside the slain Don's door
They left his daughter, as they fled :

They spared her life, because she bore
Their Chieftain's blood and name.   The red
And blood-stained hidden hoards of gold
They hollowed from the stout ship's hold,
And bore in many a slim canoe —
To where ?   The good priest only knew.

IV.

The course of life is like the sea :
Men come and go ; tides rise and fall ;
And that is all of history.
The tide flows in, flows out to-day, —
And that is all that man may say ;
Man is, man was, — and that is all.

Revenge at last came like a tide, —
'T was sweeping, deep, and terrible ;
The Christian found the land, and came
To take possession in Christ's name.
For every white man that had died
I think a thousand red men fell, —
A Christian custom ; and the land
Lay lifeless as some burned-out brand.

V.

Ere while the slain Don's daughter grew
A glorious thing, a flower of spring,
A lithe slim reed, a sun-loved weed,
A something more than mortal knew ;
A mystery of grace and face, —
A silent mystery that stood
An empress in that sea-set wood,
Supreme, imperial in her place.

It might have been men's lust for gold, —
For all men knew that lawless crew
Left hoards of gold in that ship's hold,
That drew ships hence, and silent drew
Strange Jasons to that steep wood shore,
As if to seek that hidden store, —
I never either cared or knew.

I say it might have been this gold
That ever drew and strangely drew
Strong men of land, strange men of sea,
To seek this shore of mystery
With all its wondrous tales untold :

2

The gold or her, which of the two?
It matters not; I never knew.

But this I know, that as for me,
Between that face and the hard fate
That kept me ever from my own,
As some wronged monarch from his throne,
God's heaped-up gold of land or sea
Had never weighed one feather's weight.

Her home was on the wooded height, —
A woody home, a priest at prayer,
A perfume in the fervid air,
And angels watching her at night.
I can but think upon the skies
That bound that other Paradise.

VI.

Below a star-built arch, as grand
As ever bended heaven spanned;
Tall trees like mighty columns grew —
They loomed as if to pierce the blue,
They reached as reaching heaven through.

The shadowed stream rolled far below,
Where men moved noiseless to and fro
As in some vast cathedral, when
The calm of prayer comes to men,
With benedictions, bending low.

Lo! wooded sea-banks, wild and steep!
A trackless wood; a snowy cone
That lifted from this wood alone!
This wild wide river, dark and deep!
A ship against the shore asleep!

VII.

An Indian woman crept, a crone,
Hard by about the land alone,
The relic of her perished race.
She wore rich, rudely-fashioned bands
Of gold above her bony hands:
She hissed hot curses on the place!

VIII.

Go seek the red man's last retreat!
A lonesome land, the haunted lands!

Red mouths of beasts, red men's red hands:
Red prophet-priest, in mute defeat!

His boundaries in blood are writ!
His land is ghostland!   That is his,
Whatever man may claim of this;
Beware how you shall enter it!
He stands God's guardian of ghostlands;
Ay, this same wrapped half-prophet stands
All nude and voiceless, nearer to
The awful God than I or you.

IX.

This bronzed child, by that river's brink,
Stood fair to see as you can think,
As tall as tall reeds at her feet,
As fresh as flowers in her hair;
As sweet as flowers over-sweet,
As fair as vision more than fair!

How beautiful she was!   How wild!
How pure as water-plant, this child, —

This one wild child of Nature here
Grown tall in shadows.

                And how near
To God, where no man stood between
Her eyes and scenes no man hath seen, —
This maiden that so mutely stood,
The one lone woman of that wood.

Stop still, my friend, and do not stir,
Shut close your page and think of her.
The birds sang sweeter for her face ;
Her lifted eyes were like a grace
To seamen of that solitude,
However rough, however rude.

The rippled rivers of her hair,
That ran in wondrous waves, somehow
Flowed down divided by her brow, —
Half mantled her within its care,
And flooded all, or bronze or snow,
In its uncommon fold and flow.

A perfume and an incense lay
Before her, as an incense sweet
Before blithe mowers of sweet May

In early morn. Her certain feet
Embarked on no uncertain way.

Come, think how perfect before men,
How sweet as sweet magnolia bloom
Embalmed in dews of morning, when
Rich sunlight leaps from midnight gloom
Resolved to kiss, and swift to kiss
Ere yet morn wakens man to bliss.

X.

The days swept on. Her perfect year
Was with her now. The sweet perfume
Of womanhood in holy bloom,
As when red harvest blooms appear,
Possessed her now. The priest did pray
That saints alone should pass that way.

A red bird built beneath her roof,
Brown squirrels crossed her cabin sill,
And welcome came or went at will.
A hermit spider wove his web,
And up against the roof would spin
His net to catch mosquitoes in.

The silly elk, the spotted fawn,
And all dumb beasts that came to drink,
That stealthy stole upon the brink
In that dim while that lies between
The coming night and going dawn,
On seeing her familiar face
Would fearless stop and stand in place.

She was so kind, the beasts of night
Gave her the road as if her right;
The panther crouching overhead
In sheen of moss would hear her tread
And bend his eyes, but never stir
Lest he by chance might frighten her.

Yet in her splendid strength, her eyes,
There lay the lightning of the skies;
The love-hate of the lioness,
To kill the instant, or caress:
A pent-up soul that sometimes grew
Impatient; why, she hardly knew.

At last she sighed, uprose, and threw
Her strong arms out as if to hand

Her love, sun-born and all complete
At birth, to some brave lover's feet
On some far, fair, and unseen land,
As knowing now not what to do !

XI.

How beautiful she was !   Why, she
Was inspiration !   She was born
To walk God's summer hills at morn,
Nor waste her by this wood-dark sea.
What wonder, then, her soul's white wings
Beat at its bars, like living things !

Once more she sighed !   She wandered through
The sea-bound wood, then stopped and drew
Her hand above her face, and swept
The lonesome sea, and all day kept
Her face to sea, as if she knew
Some day, some near or distant day,
Her destiny should come that way.

XII.

How proud she was !   How darkly fair !
How full of faith, of love, of strength !

Her calm, proud eyes! Her great hair's
    length, —
Her long, strong, tumbled, careless hair,
Half curled and knotted anywhere,
From brow to breast, from cheek to chin,
For love to trip and tangle in!

XIII.

At last a tall strange sail was seen:
It came so slow, so wearily,
Came creeping cautious up the sea,
As if it crept from out between
The half-closed sea and sky that lay
Tight wedged together, far away.

She watched it, wooed it. She did pray
It might not pass her by, but bring
Some love, some hate, some anything,
To break the awful loneliness
That like a nightly nightmare lay
Upon her proud and pent-up soul
Until it barely brooked control.

XIV.

The ship crept silent up the sea,
And came —

       You cannot understand
How fair she was, how sudden she
Had sprung, full-grown, to womanhood:
How gracious, yet how proud and grand;
How glorified, yet fresh and free,
How human, yet how more than good.

XV.

The ship stole slowly, slowly on ; —
Should you in Californian field
In ample flower-time behold
The soft south rose lift like a shield
Against the sudden sun at dawn,
A double handful of heaped gold,
Why you, perhaps, might understand
How splendid and how queenly she
Uprose beside that wood-set sea.

The storm-worn ship scarce seemed to creep
From wave to wave. It scarce could keep —

How still this fair girl stood, how fair !
How proud her presence as she stood
Between that vast sea and west wood !
How large and liberal her soul,
How confident, how purely chare,
How trusting; how untried the whole
Great heart, grand faith, that blossomed there !

XVI.

Ay, she was as Madonna to
The tawny, lawless, faithful few
Who touched her hand and knew her soul :
She drew them, drew them as the pole
Points all things to itself.
                          She drew
Men upward as a moon of spring,
High wheeling, vast and bosom-full,
Half clad in clouds and white as wool,
Draws all the strong seas following.

Yet still she moved as sad, as lone
As that same moon that leans above,
And seems to search high heaven through

For some strong, all-sufficient love,
For one brave love to be her own,
To lean upon, to love, to woo,
To lord her high white world, to yield
His clashing sword against her shield.

Oh, I once knew a sad, white dove
That died for such sufficient love,
Such high-born soul with wings to soar :
That stood up equal in its place,
That looked love level in the face,
Nor wearied love with leaning o'er
To lift love level where she trod
In sad delight the hills of God.

XVII.

How slow before the sleeping breeze,
That stranger ship from under seas !
How like to Dido by her sea,
When reaching arms imploringly, —
Her large, round, rich, impassioned arms,
Tossed forth from all her storied charms, —
This one lone maiden leaning stood
Above that sea, beside the wood !

The ship crept strangely up the seas;
Her shrouds seemed shreds, her masts seemed
 trees, —
Strange tattered trees of toughest bough
That knew no cease of storm till now.
The maiden pitied her; she prayed
Her crew might come, nor feel afraid;
She prayed the winds might come, — they came,
As birds that answer to a name.

The maiden held her blowing hair
That bound her beauteous self about;
The sea-winds housed within her hair:
She let it go, it blew in rout
About her bosom full and bare.
Her round, full arms were free as air,
Her high hands clasped, as clasped in prayer.

XVIII.

The breeze grew bold, the battered ship
Began to flap her weary wings;
The tall, torn masts began to dip
And walk the wave like living things.
She rounded in, she struck the stream,
She moved like some majestic dream.

The captain kept her deck.   He stood
A Hercules among his men;
And now he watched the sea, and then
He peered as if to pierce the wood.
He now looked back, as if pursued,
Now swept the sea with glass, as though
He fled or feared some hidden foe.

Swift sailing up the river's mouth,
Swift tacking north, swift tacking south,
He touched the overhanging wood;
He tacked his ship; his tall black mast
Touched tree-top mosses as he passed ;
He touched the steep shore where she stood.

XIX.

Her hands still clasped as if in prayer,
Sweet prayer set to silentness ;
Her sun-browned throat uplifted, bare
And beautiful.
                    Her eager face
Illumed with love and tenderness,
And all her presence gave such grace,

Dark shadowed in her cloud of hair,
That she seemed more than mortal fair.

XX.

He saw. He could not speak. No more
With lifted glass he sought the sea ;
No more he watched the wild new shore.
Now foes might come, now friends might flee ;
He could not speak, he would not stir, —
He saw but her, he feared but her.

The black ship ground against the shore,
She ground against the bank as one
With long and weary journeys done,
That would not rise to journey more.

Yet still this Jason silent stood
And gazed against that sun-lit wood,
As one whose soul is anywhere.

All seemed so fair, so wondrous fair !
At last aroused, he stepped to land
Like some Columbus. They laid hand
On lands and fruits, and rested there.

XXI.

He found all fairer than fair morn
In sylvan land, where waters run
With downward leap against the sun,
And full-grown sudden May is born.
He found her taller than tall corn
Tiptoe in tassel; found her sweet
As vale where bees of Hybla meet.

An unblown rose, an unread book;
A wonder in her wondrous eyes;
A large, religious, steadfast look
Of faith, of trust, — the look of one
New welcomed in her Paradise.

He read this book, — read on and on
From titlepage to colophon :
As in cool woods, some summer day,
You find delight in some sweet lay,
And so entranced read on and on
From titlepage to colophon.

XXII.

And who was he that rested there, —
This Hercules, so huge, so rare,

This giant of a grander day,
This Theseus of a nobler Greece,
This Jason of the golden fleece ?
And who was he ?   And who were they
That came to seek the hidden gold
Long hallowed from the pirate's hold?
I do not know.   You need not care.

.   .   .   .   .   .

They loved, this maiden and this man,
And that is all I surely know, —
The rest is as the winds that blow.
He bowed as brave men bow to fate,
Yet proud and resolute and bold ;
She, coy at first, and mute and cold,
Held back and seemed to hesitate, —
Half frightened at this love that ran
Hard gallop till her hot heart beat
Like sounding of swift courser's feet.

XXIII.

Two strong streams of a land must run
Together surely as the sun
Succeeds the moon.   Who shall gainsay

3

The fates that reign, that wisely reign ?
Love is, love was, shall be again.
Like death, inevitable it is ;
Perchance, like death, the dawn of bliss.
Let us, then, love the perfect day,
The twelve o'clock of life, and stop
The two hands pointing to the top,
And hold them tightly while we may.

XXIV.

How piteous strange is love !   The walks
By wooded ways ; the silent talks
Beneath the broad and fragrant bough.
The dark deep wood, the dense black dell,
Where scarce a single gold beam fell
From out the sun.

                         They rested now
On mossy trunk.   They wandered then
Where never fell the feet of men.

Then longer walks, then deeper woods,
Then sweeter talks, sufficient sweet,
In denser, deeper solitudes, —

Dear careless ways for careless feet ;
Sweet talks of paradise for two,
And only two, to watch or woo.

She rarely spake.   All seemed a dream
She would not waken from.   She lay
All night but waiting for the day,
When she might see his face, and deem
This man, with all his perils passed,
Had found the Lotus-land at last.

XXV.

The year waxed fervid, and the sun
Fell central down.   The forest lay
A-quiver in the heat.   The sea
Below the steep bank seemed to run
A molten sea of gold.
                              Away
Against the gray and rock-built isles
That broke the molten watery miles
Where lonesome sea-cows called all day,
The sudden sun smote angrily.

Therefore the need of deeper deeps,
Of denser shade for man and maid,
Of higher heights, of cooler steeps,
Where all day long the sea-wind stayed.

They sought the rock-reared steep. The breeze
Swept twenty thousand miles of seas ;
Had twenty thousand things to say
Of love, of lovers of Cathay,
To lovers 'mid these high-held trees.

XXVI.

To left, to right, below the height,
Below the wood by wave and stream,
Plumed pampas grasses grew to gleam
And bend their lordly plumes, and run
And shake, as if in very fright
Before sharp lances of the sun.

They saw the tide-bound battered ship
Creep close below against the bank ;
They saw it cringe and shrink ; it shrank
As shrinks some huge black beast with fear
When some uncommon dread is near.

They heard the melting resin drip,
As drip the last brave blood-drops when
Life's battle waxes hot with men.

XXVII.

Yet what to her were burning seas,
Or what to him was forest flame ?
They loved; they loved the glorious trees,
The gleaming tides, or rise or fall ;
They loved the lisping winds that came
From sea-lost spice-set isles unknown,
With breath not warmer than their own :
They loved, they loved, — and that was all.

XXVIII.

Full noon ! Below the ancient moss
With mighty boughs high clanged across,
The man with sweet words, over-sweet,
Fell pleading, plaintive, at her feet.

He spake of love, of boundless love, —
Of love that knew no other land,

Or face, or place, or anything;
Of love that like the wearied dove
Could light nowhere, but kept the wing
Till she alone put forth her hand,
And so received it in her ark
From seas that shake against the dark!

He clasped her hands, climbed past her knees,
Forgot her hands and kissed her hair, —
The while her two hands clasped in prayer,
And fair face lifted to the trees.

Her proud breast heaved, her pure proud breast
Rose like the waves in their unrest
When counter storms possess the seas.
Her mouth, her arched, uplifted mouth,
Her ardent mouth that thirsted so, —
No glowing love-song of the South
Can say; no man can say or know
The glory there, and so live on
Content without that glory gone!

Her face still lifted up.   And she
Disdained the cup of passion he
Hard pressed her panting lips to touch.

She dashed it by despised, and she
Caught fast her breath.   She trembled much,
And sudden rose full height, and stood
An empress in high womanhood :
She stood a tower, tall as when
Proud Roman mothers suckled men
Of old-time truth and taught them such.

XXIX.

Her soul surged vast as space is.   She
Was trembling as a courser when
His thin flank quivers, and his feet
Touch velvet on the turf, and he
Is all afoam, alert, and fleet
As sunlight glancing on the sea,
And full of triumph before men.

At last she bended some her face,
Half leaned, then put him back a pace,
And met his eyes.
                    Calm, silently
Her eyes looked deep into his eyes, —
As maidens down some mossy well

Do peer in hope by chance to tell
By image there what future lies
Before them, and what face shall be
The pole-star of their destiny.

Pure Nature's lover !   Loving him
With love that made all pathways dim
And difficult where he was not, —
Then marvel not at form forgot.
And who shall chide ?   Doth priest know aught
Of sign, or holy unction brought
From over seas, that ever can
Make man love maid or maid love man
One whit the more, one bit the less,
For all his mummeries to bless ?
Yea, all his blessing or his ban ?

The winds breathed warm as Araby :
She leaned upon his breast, she lay
A wide-winged swan with folded wing.
He drowned his hot face in her hair,
He heard her great heart rise and sing ;
He felt her bosom swell.
                              The air
Swooned sweet with perfume of her form.

Her breast was warm, her breath was warm,
And warm her warm and perfumed mouth
As summer journeys through the South.

XXX.

The argent sea surged steep below,
Surged languid in a tropic glow ;
And two great hearts kept surging so !

The fervid kiss of heaven lay
Precipitate on wood and sea.
Two great souls glowed with ecstasy,
The sea glowed scarce as warm as they.

XXXI.

'T was love's low amber afternoon.
Two far-off pheasants thrummed a tune,
A cricket clanged a restful air.
The dreamful billows beat a rune
Like heart regrets.
                    Around her head
There shone a halo.   Men have said

'T was from a dash of Titian
That flooded all her storm of hair
In gold and glory.   But they knew,
Yea, all men know there ever grew
A halo round about her head
Like sunlight scarcely vanishèd.

XXXII.

How still she was !   She only knew
His love.   She saw no life beyond.
She loved with love that only lives
Outside itself and selfishness, —
A love that glows in its excess ;
A love that melts pure gold, and gives
Thenceforth to all who come to woo
No coins but this face stamped thereon, —
Ay, this one image stamped upon
Its face, with some dim date long gone.

XXXIII.

They kept the headland high ; the ship
Below began to chafe her chain,

To groan as some great beast in pain;
While white fear leapt from lip to lip:
"The woods are fire! the woods are flame!
Come down and save us, in God's name!"

He heard! he did not speak or stir, —
He thought of her, of only her.
While flames behind, before them lay
To hold the stoutest heart at bay!

Strange sounds were heard far up the flood, —
Strange, savage sounds that chilled the blood!
Then sudden from the dense dark wood
Above, about them where they stood
A thousand beasts came peering out;
And now was thrust a long black snout,
And now a tusky mouth.　It was
A sight to make the stoutest pause.

"Cut loose the ship!" the black mate cried;
"Cut loose the ship!" the crew replied.
They drove into the sea.　It lay
As light as ever middle day.

The while their half-blind bitch, that sat
All slobber-mouthed, and monkish cowled
With great, broad, floppy, leathern ears,
Amid the men, rose up and howled,
And doleful howled her plaintive fears,
While all looked mute aghast thereat.
It was the grimmest eve, I think,
That ever hung on Hades' brink.

Great broad-winged bats possessed the air,
Bats whirling blindly everywhere;
It was such troubled twilight eve
As never mortal would believe.

XXXIV.

Some say the crazed hag lit the wood
In circle where the lovers stood;
Some say the gray priest feared the crew
Might find at last the hoard of gold
Long hidden from the black ship's hold, —
I doubt me if men ever knew.
But such mad, howling, flame-lit shore
No mortal ever saw before.

Huge beasts above that shining sea,
Wild, hideous beasts with shaggy hair,
With red mouths lifting in the air,
They piteous howled, and plaintively, —
The wildest sounds, the weirdest sight
That ever shook the walls of night.

How lorn they howled, with lifted head,
To dim and distant isles that lay
Wedged tight along a line of red,
Caught in the closing gates of day
'Twixt sky and sea and far away, —
It was the saddest sound to hear
That ever struck on human ear.

They doleful called; and answered they
The plaintive sea-cows far away, —
The great sea-cows that called from isles,
Away across wide watery miles,
With dripping mouths and lolling tongue,
As if they called for captured young, —

The huge sea-cows that called the whiles
Their great wide mouths were mouthing moss;
And still they doleful called across

From isles beyond the watery miles.
No sound can half so doleful be
As sea-cows calling from the sea.

XXXV.

The drowned sun sank and died.   He lay
In seas of blood.   He sinking drew
The gates of sunset sudden to,
Where shattered day in fragments lay,
And night came, moving in mad flame :
The night came, lighted as he came,
As lighted by high summer sun
Descending through the burning blue.
It was a gold and amber hue,
And all hues blended into one.
The night spilled splendor where she came,
And filled the yellow world with flame.

The moon came on, came leaning low
Along the far sea-isles aglow ;
She fell along that amber flood
A silver flame in seas of blood.

It was the strangest moon, ah me !
That ever settled on God's sea.

XXXVI.

Slim snakes slid down from fern and grass,
From wood, from fen, from anywhere ;
You could not step, you would not pass,
And you would hesitate to stir,
Lest in some sudden, hurried tread
Your foot struck some unbruisèd head :

They slid in streams into the stream, —
It seemed like some infernal dream ;
They curved, and graceful curved across,
Like graceful, waving sea-green moss, —
There is no art of man can make
A ripple like a rippling snake !

XXXVII.

Abandoned, lorn, the lovers stood,
Abandoned there, death in the air !
That beetling steep, that blazing wood, —
Red flame ! and red flame everywhere !

Yet was he born to strive, to bear
The front of battle.   He would die
In noble effort, and defy
The grizzled visage of despair.

He threw his two strong arms full length
As if to surely test their strength ;
Then tore his vestments, textile things
That could but tempt the demon wings
Of flame that girt them round about,
Then threw his garments to the air
As one that laughed at death, at doubt,
And like a god stood grand and bare.

She did not hesitate ; she knew
The need of action ; swift she threw
Her burning vestments by, and bound
Her wondrous wealth of hair that fell
An all-concealing cloud around
Her glorious presence, as he came
To seize and bear her through the flame, —
An Orpheus out of burning hell !

He leaned above her, wound his arm
About her splendor, while the noon

Of flood-tide, manhood, flushed his face,
And high flames leapt the high headland ! —
They stood as twin-hewn statues stand,
High lifted in some storied place.

He clasped her close, he spoke of death, —
Of death and love in the same breath.
He clasped her close ; her bosom lay
Like ship safe anchored in some bay.

XXXVIII.

The flames !   They could not stand or stay ;
Before the beetling steep, the sea !
But at his feet a narrow way,
A short steep path, pitched suddenly
Safe open to the river's beach,
Where lay a small white isle in reach, —
A small, white, rippled isle of sand
Where yet the two might safely land.

And there, through smoke and flame, behold
The priest stood safe, yet all appalled !
He reached the cross ; he cried, he called ;
He waved his high-held cross of gold.

4

He called and called, he bade them fly
Through flames to him, nor bide and die!

Her lover saw; he saw, and knew
His giant strength would bear her through.
And yet he would not start or stir.
He clasped her close as death can hold,
Or dying miser clasp his gold, —
His hold became a part of her.

He would not give her up!   He would
Not bear her waveward though he could!
That height was heaven; the wave was hell.
He clasped her close, — what else had done
The manliest man beneath the sun?
Was it not well? was it not well?

O man, be glad! be grandly glad,
And kinglike walk thy ways of death!
For more than years of bliss you had
That one brief time you breathed her breath.
Yea, more than years upon a throne
That one brief time you held her fast,
Soul surged to soul, vehement, vast, —
True breast to breast, and all your own.

Live me one day, one narrow night,
One second of supreme delight
Like that, and I will blow like chaff
The hollow years aside, and laugh
A loud triumphant laugh, and I,
King-like and crowned, will gladly die.

Oh, but to wrap my love with flame!
With flame within, with flame without!
Oh, but to die like this, nor doubt —
To die and know her still the same!
To know that down the ghostly shore
Snow-white she waits me evermore!

XXXIX.

He poised her, held her high in air, —
His great strong limbs, his great arm's length!—
Then turned his knotted shoulders bare
As birth-time in his splendid strength,
And strode, strode with a lordly stride
To where the high and wood-hung edge
Looked down, far down upon the molten tide.
The flames leapt with him to the ledge,
The flames leapt leering at his side.

XL.

He leaned above the ledge.   Below
He saw the black ship idly cruise, —
A midge below, a mile below.
His limbs were knotted as the thews
Of Hercules in his death-throe.

The flame! the flame! the envious flame!
She wound her arms, she wound her hair
About his tall form, grand and bare,
To stay the fierce flame where it came.

The black ship, like some moonlit wreck,
Below along the burning sea
Crept on and on all silently,
With silent pygmies on her deck.

That midge-like ship far, far below;
That mirage lifting from the hill!
His flame-lit form began to grow, —
To grow and grow more grandly still.
The ship so small, that form so tall,
It grew to tower over all.

A tall Colossus, bronze and gold,
As if that flame-lit form were he

Who once bestrode the Rhodian sea,
And ruled the watery world of old:
As if the lost Colossus stood
Above that burning sea of wood.

And she, that shapely form upheld,
Held high, as if to touch the sky,
What airy shape, how shapely high, —
A goddess of the seas of eld!

Her hand upheld, her high right hand,
As if she would forget the land;
As if to gather stars, and heap
The stars like torches there to light
Her Hero's path across the deep
To some far isle that fearful night.

It was as if Colossus came,
Came proudly reaching from the flame
Above the sea in sheen of gold,
His sea-bride leaping from his hold;
The lost Colossus, and his bride
In bronze perfection at his side:
As if the lost Colossus came

Companioned from the past, his bride
With torch all faithful at his side :

With star-tipped torch that reached and rolled
Through cloud-built corridors of gold :
His bride, austere and stern and grand, —
Bartholdi's goddess by the sea,
Far lifting, lighting Liberty
From prison seas to Freedom's land.

XLI.

The flame ! the envious flame, it leapt
Enraged to see such majesty,
Such scorn of death ; such kingly scorn.
Then like some lightning-riven tree
They sank down in that flame — and slept
And all was hushed above that steep
So still, that they might sleep and sleep ;
As still as when a day is born.

At last ! from out the embers leapt
Two shafts of light above the night, —
Two wings of flame that lifting swept
In steady, calm, and upward flight ;

Two wings of flame against the white
Far-lifting, tranquil, snowy cone;
Two wings of love, two wings of light,
Far, far above that troubled night,
As mounting, mounting to God's throne.

XLII.

And all night long that upward light
Lit up the sea-cow's bed below:
The far sea-cows still calling so
It seemed as they must call all night.
All night! there was no night.   Nay, nay,
There was no night.   The night that lay
Between that awful eve and day,—
That nameless night was burned away.

THE RHYME OF THE GREAT RIVER.

PART I.

THE RHYME OF THE GREAT RIVER.

PART I.

RHYME on, rhyme on in reedy flow,
O river, rhymer ever sweet !
The story of thy land is meet,
The stars stand listening to know.

Rhyme on, O river of the earth !
Gray father of the dreadful seas,
Rhyme on ! the world upon its knees
Shall yet invoke thy wealth and worth.

Rhyme on, the reed is at thy mouth,
O kingly minstrel, mighty stream !
Thy Crescent City, like a dream,
Hangs in the heaven of my South.

Rhyme on, rhyme on ! these broken strings
  Sing sweetest in this warm south wind ;
  I sit thy willow banks and bind
A broken harp that fitful sings.

I.

AND where is my city, sweet blossom-sown
    town?
And what is her glory, and what has she done?
By the Mexican seas in the path of the sun
Sit you down: in the crescent of seas sit you down.

Ay, glory enough by my Mexican seas!
    Ay, story enough in that battle-torn town,
    Hidden down in the crescent of seas, hidden
        down
'Mid mantle and sheen of magnolia-strown trees.

But mine is the story of souls; of a soul
    That bartered God's limitless kingdom for
        gold, —
    Sold stars and all space for a thing he could
        hold
In his palm for a day, ere he hid with the
    mole.

O father of waters ! O river so vast !
   So deep, so strong, and so wondrous wild, —
He embraces the land as he rushes past,
   Like a savage father embracing his child.

His sea-land is true and so valiantly true,
   His leaf-land is fair and so marvellous fair,
   His palm-land is filled with a perfumed air
Of magnolia blooms to its dome of blue.

His rose-land has arbors of moss-swept oak, —
   Gray, Druid old oaks ; and the moss that sways
And swings in the wind is the battle-smoke
   Of duellists, dead in her storied days.

His love-land has churches and bells and chimes ;
   His love-land has altars and orange flowers ;
And that is the reason for all these rhymes, —
   These bells, they are ringing through all the
      hours !

His sun-land has churches, and priests at prayer,
   White nuns, as white as the far north snow ;
   They go where danger may bid them go, —
They dare when the angel of death is there.

His love-land has ladies so fair, so fair,
  In the Creole quarter, with great black eyes, —
So fair that the Mayor must keep them there
  Lest troubles, like troubles of Troy, arise.

His love-land has ladies, with eyes held down, —
  Held down, because if they lifted them,
Why, you would be lost in that old French town,
  Though you held even to God's garment hem.

His love-land has ladies so fair, so fair,
  That they bend their eyes to the holy book
Lest you should forget yourself, your prayer,
  And never more cease to look and to look.

And these are the ladies that no men see,
  And this is the reason men see them not.
Better their modest sweet mystery, —
  Better by far than the battle-shot.

And so, in this curious old town of tiles,
  The proud French quarter of days long gone,
In castles of Spain and tumble-down piles
  These wonderful ladies live on and on.

I sit in the church where they come and go;
  I dream of glory that has long since gone,
Of the low raised high, of the high brought low,
  As in battle-torn days of Napoleon.

These piteous places, so rich, so poor!
  One quaint old church at the edge of the town
Has white tombs laid to the very church door, —
  White leaves in the story of life turned down.

White leaves in the story of life are these,
  The low white slabs in the long strong grass,
  Where Glory has emptied her hour-glass
And dreams with the dreamers beneath the trees.

I dream with the dreamers beneath the sod,
  Where souls pass by to the great white throne;
  I count each tomb as a mute milestone
For weary, sweet souls on their way to God.

I sit all day by the vast, strong stream,
  'Mid low white slabs in the long strong grass
  Where Time has forgotten for aye to pass,
To dream, and ever to dream and to dream.

This quaint old church with its dead to the door,
 By the cypress swamp at the edge of the town,
 So restful seems that you want to sit down
And rest you, and rest you for evermore.

And one white tomb is a lowliest tomb,
 That has crept up close to the crumbling door,—
Some penitent soul, as imploring room
 Close under the cross that is leaning o'er.

'T is a low white slab, and 't is nameless, too —
 Her untold story, why, who should know?
Yet God, I reckon, can read right through
 That nameless stone to the bosom below.

And the roses know, and they pity her, too;
 They bend their heads in the sun or rain,
 And they read, and they read, and then read
  again,
As children reading strange pictures through.

Why, surely her sleep it should be profound;
 For oh the apples of gold above!
 And oh the blossoms of bridal love!
And oh the roses that gather around!

5

The sleep of a night, or a thousand morns?
　　Why what is the difference here, to-day?
　　Sleeping and sleeping the years away
With all earth's roses, and none of its thorns.

Magnolias white and the roses red —
　　The palm-tree here and the cypress there:
Sit down by the palm at the feet of the dead,
　　And hear a penitent's midnight prayer.

II.

The old churchyard is still as death,
　　A stranger passes to and fro
　　As if to church — he does not go —
The dead night does not draw a breath.

A lone sweet lady prays within.
　　The stranger passes by the door —
　　Will he not pray?　Is he so poor
He has no prayer for his sin?

Is he so poor ! His two strong hands
 Are full and heavy, as with gold ;
They clasp, as clasp two iron bands
 About two bags with eager hold.

Will he not pause and enter in,
 Put down his heavy load and rest,
Put off his garmenting of sin,
 As some black burden from his breast ?

Ah, me ! the brave alone can pray.
 The church-door is as cannon's mouth
 To sinner North, or sinner South,
More dreaded than dread battle day.

Now two men pace. They pace apart,
 And one with youth and truth is fair ;
The fervid sun is in his heart,
 The tawny South is in his hair.

Ay, two men pace, pace left and right —
 The lone, sweet lady prays within —
Ay, two men pace : the silent night
 Kneels down in prayer for some sin.

Lo! two men pace; and one is gray,
   A blue-eyed man from snow-clad land,
   With something heavy in each hand, —
With heavy feet, as feet of clay.

Ay, two men pace; and one is light
   Of step, but still his brow is dark
   His eyes are as a kindled spark
That burns beneath the brow of night!

And still they pace.   The stars are red,
   The tombs are white as frosted snow;
The silence is as if the dead
   Did pace in couples, to and fro.

III.

The azure curtain of God's house
   Draws back, and hangs star-pinned to
      space;
I hear the low, large moon arouse,
   I see her lift her languid face.

I see her shoulder up the east,
   Low-necked, and large as womanhood, —

Low-necked, as for some ample feast
   Of gods, within yon orange-wood.

She spreads white palms, she whispers peace, —
   Sweet peace on earth for evermore ;
Sweet peace for two beneath the trees,
   Sweet peace for one within the door.

The bent stream, like a scimitar
   Flashed in the sun, sweeps on and on,
   Till sheathed like some great sword new-drawn
In seas beneath the Carib's star.

The high moon climbs the sapphire hill,
   The lone sweet lady prays within ;
   The crickets keep a clang and din —
They are so loud, earth is so still !

And two men glare in silence there !
   The bitter, jealous hate of each
   Has grown too deep for deed or speech —
The lone, sweet lady keeps her prayer.

The vast moon high through heaven's field
   In circling chariot is rolled ;

The golden stars are spun and reeled,
  And woven into cloth of gold.

The white magnolia fills the night
  With perfume, as the proud moon fills
The glad earth with her ample light
  From out her awful sapphire hills.

White orange blossoms fill the boughs
  Above, about the old church door, —
They wait the bride, the bridal vows, —
  They never hung so fair before.

The two men glare as dark as sin!
  And yet all seems so fair, so white,
  You would not reckon it was night, —
The while the lady prays within.

IV.

She prays so very long and late, —
  The two men, weary, waiting there, —
The great magnolia at the gate
  Bends drowsily above her prayer.

The cypress in his cloak of moss,
   That watches on in silent gloom,
Has leaned and shaped a shadow-cross
   Above the nameless, lowly tomb.

What can she pray for ?   What her sin ?
   What folly of a maid so fair ?
   What shadows bind the wondrous hair
Of one who prays so long within ?

The palm-trees guard in regiment,
   Stand right and left without the gate ;
   The myrtle-moss trees wait and wait ;
The tall magnolia leans intent.

The cypress trees, on gnarled old knees,
   Far out the dank and marshy deep
   Where slimy monsters groan and creep,
Kneel with her in their marshy seas.

What can her sin be ?   Who shall know ?
   The night flies by, — a bird on wing ;
The men no longer to and fro
   Stride up and down, or anything.

For one so weary and so old
   Has hardly strength to stride or stir;
He can but hold his bags of gold, —
   But hug his gold and wait for her.

The two stand still, — stand face to face.
   The moon slides on ; the midnight air
   Is perfumed as a house of prayer —
The maiden keeps her holy place.

Two men !   And one is gray, but one
   Scarce lifts a full-grown face as yet :
   With light foot on life's threshold set, —
Is he the other's sun-born son ?

And one is of the land of snow,
   And one is of the land of sun ;
   A black-eyed burning youth is one,
But one has pulses cold and slow :

Ay, cold and slow from clime of snow
   Where Nature's bosom, icy bound,
   Holds all her forces, hard, profound, —
Holds close where all the South lets go.

Blame not the sun, blame not the snows;
   God's great schoolhouse for all is clime,
   The great school-teacher, Father Time;
And each has borne as best he knows.

At last the elder speaks, — he cries, —
   He speaks as if his heart would break;
He speaks out as a man that dies, —
   As dying for some lost love's sake:

" Come, take this bag of gold, and go!
   Come, take one bag! See, I have two!
Oh, why stand silent, staring so,
   When I would share my gold with you?

" Come, take this gold! See how I pray!
   See how I bribe, and beg, and buy, —
Ay, buy! buy love, as you, too, may
   Some day before you come to die.

" God! take this gold, I beg, I pray!
   I beg as one who thirsting cries
   For but one drop of drink, and dies
In some lone, loveless desert way.

" You hesitate ? Still hesitate ?
　　Stand silent still and mock my pain ?
Still mock to see me wait and wait,
　　And wait her love, as earth waits rain ? ''

V.

O broken ship !　O starless shore !
　　O black and everlasting night,
Where love comes never any more
　　To light man's way with heaven's light.

A godless man with bags of gold
　　I think a most unholy sight ;
　　Ah, who so desolate at night
Amid death's sleepers still and cold ?

A godless man on holy ground
　　I think a most unholy sight.
I hear death trailing like a hound
　　Hard after him, and swift to bite.

VI.

The vast moon settles to the west:
  Two men beside a nameless tomb,
And one would sit thereon to rest, —
  Ay, rest below, if there were room.

What is this rest of death, sweet friend?
  What is the rising up, — and where?
  I say, death is a lengthened prayer,
A longer night, a larger end.

Hear you the lesson I once learned:
  I died; I sailed a million miles
  Through dreamful, flowery, restful isles, —
She was not there, and I returned.

I say the shores of death and sleep
  Are one; that when we, wearied, come
  To Lethe's waters, and lie dumb,
'T is death, not sleep, holds us to keep.

Yea, we lie dead for need of rest
  And so the soul drifts out and o'er
  The vast still waters to the shore
Beyond, in pleasant, tranquil quest:

It sails straight on, forgetting pain,
　　Past isles of peace, to perfect rest, —
　　'Now were it best abide, or best
Return and take up life again ?

And that is all of death there is,
　　Believe me. If you find your love
　　In that far land, then like the dove
Abide, and turn not back to this.

But if you find your love not there;
　　Or if your feet feel sure, and you
　　Have still allotted work to do, —
Why, then return to toil and care.

Death is no mystery. 'T is plain
　　If death be mystery, then sleep
　　Is mystery thrice strangely deep, —
For oh this coming back again !

Austerest ferryman of souls !
　　I see the gleam of solid shores,
　　I hear thy steady stroke of oars
Above the wildest wave that rolls.

O Charon, keep thy sombre ships!
  We come, with neither myrrh nor balm,
  Nor silver piece in open palm,
But lone white silence on our lips.

VII.

She prays so long! she prays so late!
  What sin in all this flower-land
  Against her supplicating hand
Could have in heaven any weight?

Prays she for her sweet self alone?
  Prays she for some one far away,
  Or some one near and dear to-day,
Or some poor, lorn, lost soul unknown?

It seems to me a selfish thing
  To pray forever for one's self;
  It seems to me like heaping pelf
In heaven by hard reckoning.

Why, I would rather stoop, and bear
  My load of sin, and bear it well
  And bravely down to burning hell,
Than ever pray one selfish prayer!

VIII.

The swift chameleon in the gloom —
    This silence it is so profound ! —
    Forsakes its bough, glides to the ground,
Then up, and lies across the tomb.

It erst was green as olive-leaf,
    It then grew gray as myrtle moss
    The time it slid the moss across ;
But now 't is marble-white with grief.

The little creature's hues are gone ;
    Here in the pale and ghostly light
    It lies so pale, so panting white, —
White as the tomb it lies upon.

The two men by that nameless tomb,
    And both so still !   You might have said
    These two men, they are also dead,
And only waiting here for room.

How still beneath the orange-bough !
    How tall was one, how bowed was one !
    The one was as a journey done,
The other as beginning now.

And one was young, — young with that youth
Eternal that belongs to truth ;
And one was old, — old with the years
That follow fast on doubts and fears.

And yet the habit of command
  Was his, in every stubborn part ;
  No common knave was he at heart,
Nor his the common coward's hand.

He looked the young man in the face,
  So full of hate, so frank of hate ;
The other, standing in his place,
  Stared back as straight and hard as fate.

And now he sudden turned away,
  And now he paced the path, and now
Came back, beneath the orange-bough
  Pale-browed, with lips as cold as clay.

As mute as shadows on a wall,
  As silent still, as dark as they,
  Before that stranger, bent and gray,
The youth stood scornful, proud, and tall.

He stood, a tall palmetto-tree
   With Spanish daggers guarding it;
   Nor deed, nor word, to him seemed fit
While she prayed on so silently.

He slew his rival with his eyes;
   His eyes were daggers piercing deep,—
   So deep that blood began to creep
From their deep wounds and drop wordwise:

His eyes so black, so bright that they
Might raise the dead, the living slay,
If but the dead, the living, bore
Such hearts as heroes had of yore:

Two deadly arrows barbed in black,
   And feathered, too, with raven's wing;
   Two arrows that could silent sting,
And with a death-wound answer back.

How fierce he was! how deadly still
   In that mesmeric, hateful stare
   Turned on the pleading stranger there
That drew to him, despite his will:

So like a bird down-fluttering,
  Down, down, beneath a snake's bright eyes,
He stood, a fascinated thing,
  That hopeless, unresisting, dies.

He raised a hard hand as before,
  Reached out the gold, and offered it
  With hand that shook as ague-fit, —
The while the youth but scorned the more.

' You will not touch it ?   In God's name
  Who are you, and what are you, then ?
Come, take this gold, and be of men, —
  A human form with human aim.

" Yea, take this gold, — she must be mine
  She shall be mine ! I do not fear
  Your scowl, your scorn, your soul austere,
The living, dead, or your dark sign.

" I saw her as she entered there ;
  I saw her, and uncovered stood :
  The perfume of her womanhood
Was holy incense on the air.

6

"She left behind sweet sanctity,
  Religion lay the way she went;
  I cried I would repent, repent !
She passed on, all unheeding me.

"Her soul is young, her eyes are bright
  And gladsome, as mine own are dim ;
  But, oh, I felt my senses swim
The time she passed me by to-night ! —

"The time she passed, nor raised her eyes
  To hear me cry I would repent,
Nor turned her head to hear my cries,
  But swifter went the way she went, —

"Went swift as youth, for all these years !
And this the strangest thing appears,
That lady there seems just the same, —
Sweet Gladys —   Ah ! you know her name ?

"You hear her name and start that I
  Should name her dear name trembling so ?
Why, boy, when I shall come to die
  That name shall be the last I know.

" That name shall be the last sweet name
    My lips shall utter in this life!
That name is brighter than bright flame, —
    That lady is my wedded wife!

" Ah, start and catch your burning breath!
    Ah, start and clutch your deadly knife!
If this be death, then be it death, —
    But that loved lady is my wife!

" Yea, you are stunned! your face is white,
    That I should come confronting you,
As comes a lorn ghost of the night
    From out the past, and to pursue.

" You thought me dead? You shake your head,
    You start back horrified to know
That she is loved, that she is wed,
    That you have sinned in loving so.

" Yet what seems strange, that lady there,
    Housed in the holy house of prayer,
Seems just the same for all her tears, —
    For all my absent twenty years.

" Yea, twenty years to-night, to-night,
 Just twenty years this day, this hour,
 Since first I plucked that perfect flower,
And not one witness of the rite.

" Nay, do not doubt, — I tell you true !
 Her prayers, her tears, her constancy
 Are all for me, are all for me, —
And not one single thought for you !

" I knew, I knew she would be here
 This night of nights to pray for me !
 And how could I for twenty year
 Know this same night so certainly ?

" Ah me ! some thoughts that we would drown
 Stick closer than a brother to
 The conscience, and pursue, pursue
Like baying hound to hunt us down.

" And then, that date is history ;
 For on that night this shore was shelled,
 And many a noble mansion felled,
With many a noble family.

" I wore the blue ; I watched the flight
  Of shells like stars tossed through the air
  To blow your hearth-stones — anywhere,
That wild, illuminated night.

" Nay, rage befits you not so well :
  Why, you were but a babe at best,
Your cradle some sharp bursted shell
  That tore, maybe, your mother's breast !

" Hear me ! We came in honored war.
  The risen world was on your track !
  The whole North-land was at our back,
From Hudson's bank to the North star !

" And from the North to palm-set sea
  The splendid fiery cyclone swept.
  Your fathers fell, your mothers wept,
Their nude babes clinging to the knee.

" A wide and desolated track :
  Behind, a path of ruin lay ;
  Before, some women by the way
Stood mutely gazing, clad in black.

" From silent women waiting there
　　Some tears came down like still small rain ;
　　Their own sons on the battle plain
Were now but viewless ghosts of air.

" Their own dear daring boys in gray, —
　　They should not see them any more ;
　　Our cruel drums kept telling o'er
The time their own sons went away.

" Through burning town, by bursting shell —
　　Yea, I remember well that night ;
　　I led through orange-lanes of light,
As through some hot outpost of hell !

That night of rainbow-shot and shell
　　Sent from your surging river's breast
　　To waken me, no more to rest, —
That night I should remember well !

That night amid the maimed and dead, —
　　A night in history set down
　　By light of many a burning town,
And written all across in red, —

" Her father dead, her brothers dead,
  Her home in flames, — what else could she
  But fly all helpless here to me,
A fluttered dove, that night of dread ?

"Short time, hot time had I to woo
  Amid the red shells' battle-chime ;
  But women rarely reckon time,
And perils speed their love when true.

" And then I wore a captain's sword ;
  And, too, had oftentime before
  Doffed cap at her dead father's door,
And passed a soldier's pleasant word.

" And then — ah, I was comely then !
  I bore no load upon my back,
  I heard no hounds upon my track,
But stood the tallest of tall men.

" Her father's and her mother's shrine,
  This church amid the orange wood,
  So near and so secure it stood,
It seemed to beckon as a sign.

" Its white cross seemed to beckon me :
　　My heart was strong, and it was mine
　To throw myself upon my knee,
　　To beg to lead her to this shrine.

" She did consent.　Through lanes of light
　I led through that church-door that night —
　Let fall your hand !　Take back your face
　And stand, — stand patient in your place !

" She loved me ; and she loves me still.
　　Yea, she clung close to me that hour
　　As honey-bee to honey-flower, —
　And still is mine, through good or ill.

" The priest stood there.　He spake the prayer ;
　　He made the holy, mystic sign.
　　And she was mine, was wholly mine, —
　Is mine this moment I will swear !

" Then days, then nights, of vast delight, —
　　Then came a doubtful, later day ;
　　The faithful priest, now far away,
　Watched with the dying in the fight :

" The priest amid the dying, dead,
　　Kept duty on the battle-field , —
　　That midnight marriage unrevealed
Kept strange thoughts running through my head.

" At last a stray ball struck the priest:
　　This vestibule his chancel was.
　　And now none lived to speak her cause,
Record, or champion her the least.

" Hear me!　I had been bred to hate
　　All priests, their mummeries and all.
　　Ah, it was fate, — ah, it was fate
That all things tempted me to fall !

" And then the rattling songs we sang
　　Those nights when rudely revelling, —
　　The songs that only soldiers sing, —
Until the very tent-poles rang !

" What is the rhyme that rhymers say
　　Of maidens born to be betrayed
　　By epaulettes and shining blade,
While soldiers love and ride away ?

" And then my comrades spake her name
  Half taunting, with a touch of shame ;
  Taught me to hold that lily-flower
  As some light pastime of the hour.

" And then the ruin in the land,
    The death, dismay, the lawlessness !
  Men gathered gold on every hand, —
    Heaped gold : and why should I do less ?

" The cry for gold was in the air,
    For Creole gold, for precious things ;
  The sword kept prodding here and there
    Through bolts and sacred fastenings.

" 'Get gold ! get gold !'   This was the cry.
  And I loved gold.   What else could I
  Or you, or any earnest one
  Born in this getting age have done ?

" With this one lesson taught from youth,
    And ever taught us, to get gold, —
    To get and hold, and ever hold, —
  What else could I have done, forsooth ?

" She, seeing how I sought for gold, —
  This girl, my wife, one late night told
  Of treasures hidden close at hand,
  In her dead father's mellow land :

" Of gold she helped her brothers hide
    Beneath a broad banana tree,
  The day the two in battle died, —
    The night she dying fled to me.

" It seemed too good ; I laughed to scorn
    Her trustful tale.   She answered not ;
  But meekly on the morrow morn
    Two massive bags of bright gold brought.

" And when she brought this gold to me,
    Red Creole gold, rich, rare, and old, —
  When I at last had gold, sweet gold,
  I cried in very ecstasy !

" Red gold ! rich gold ! two bags of gold !
    The two stout bags of gold she brought
    And gave with scarce a second thought, —
  Why, her two hands could hardly hold !

"Now I had gold ! two bags of gold !
   Two wings of gold to fly, and fly
   The wide world's girth ; red gold to hold
Against my heart for aye and aye !

"My country's lesson : ' Gold ! get gold ! '
   I learned it well in land of snow ;
   And what can glow, so brightly glow,
Long winter nights of Northern cold ?

"Ay, now at last, at last I had
   The one thing, all fair things above
   My land had taught me most to love !
A miser now ! and I grew mad.

"With those two bags of gold my own,
   I then began to plan that night
   For flight, for far and sudden flight, —
For flight ; and, too, for flight alone.

"I feared ! I feared ! My heart grew cold, —
   Some one might claim this gold of me !
   I feared her, — feared her purity,
Feared all things but my bags of gold.

" I grew to hate her face, her creed, —
    That face the fairest ever yet
That bowed o'er holy cross or bead,
    Or yet was in God's image set.

" I fled, — nay, not so knavish low
    As you have fancied, did I fly ;
I sought her at that shrine, and I
    Told her full frankly I should go.

" I stood a giant in my power, —
    And did she question or dispute ?
I stood a savage, selfish brute, —
She bowed her head, a lily-flower.

"And when I sudden turned to go,
    And told her I should come no more,
She bowed her head so low, so low,
    Her vast black hair fell pouring o'er.

" And that was all; her splendid face
    Was mantled from me, and her night
Of hair half hid her from my sight
    As she fell moaning in her place.

" And there, 'mid her dark night of hair,
　　She sobbed, low moaning through her tears,
　　That she would wait, wait all the years, —
Would wait and pray in her despair.

" Nay, did not murmur, not deny, —
　　She did not cross me one sweet word !
　　I turned and fled : I thought I heard
A night-bird's piercing low death-cry ! "

THE RHYME OF THE GREAT RIVER.

PART II.

HOW soft this moonlight of the South!
  How sweet my South in soft moonlight!
I want to kiss her warm sweet mouth
  As she lies sleeping here to-night.

How still! I do not hear a mouse.
  I see some bursting buds appear;
  I hear God in His garden, — hear
Him trim some flowers for His house.

I hear some singing stars; the mouth
  Of my vast river sings and sings,
  And pipes on reeds of pleasant things, —
Of splendid promise for my South:

My great South-woman, soon to rise
And tiptoe up and loose her hair;
Tiptoe, and take from all the skies
God's stars and glorious moon to wear!

I.

THE poet shall create or kill,
  Bid heroes live, bid braggarts die.
I look against a lurid sky, —
  My silent South lies proudly still.

The lurid light of burning lands
  Still climbs to God's house overhead;
Mute women wring white withered hands;
  Their eyes are red, their skies are red.

Poor man! still boast your bitter wars!
  Still burn and burn, and burning die.
But God's white finger spins the stars
  In calm dominion of the sky.

And not one ray of light the less
  Comes down to bid the grasses spring;
  No drop of dew nor anything
Shall fail for all your bitterness.

The land that nursed a nation's youth,
　　Ye burned it, sacked it, sapped it dry.
Ye gave it falsehoods for its truth,
　　And fame was fashioned from a lie.

If man grows large, is God the less?
　　The moon shall rise and set the same,
　　The great sun spill his splendid flame
And clothe the world in queenliness.

And from that very soil ye trod
　　Some large-souled seeing youth shall come
　　Some day, and he shall not be dumb
Before the awful court of God.

II.

The weary moon had turned away,
　　The far North-Star was turning pale
　　To hear the stranger's boastful tale
Of blood and flame that battle day.

And yet again the two men glared,
　　Close face to face above that tomb;
　　Each seemed as jealous of the room
The other eager waiting shared.

Again the man began to say,—
   As taking up some broken thread,
   As talking to the patient dead,—
The Creole was as still as they:

" That night we burned yon grass-grown town,—
   The grasses, vines are reaching up;
The ruins they are reaching down,
   As sun-browned soldiers when they sup.

" I knew her,— knew her constancy.
   She said, this night of every year
   She here would come, and kneeling here,
Would pray the live-long night for me.

" This praying seems a splendid thing!
   It drives old Time the other way;
It makes him lose all reckoning
   Of years that pagans have to pay.

" This praying seems a splendid thing!
   It makes me stronger as she prays —
   But oh the bitter, bitter days
When I became a banished thing!

" I fled, took ship, — I fled as far
  As far ships drive tow'rd the North-Star;
  For I did hate the South, the sun
  That made me think what I had done.

" I could not see a fair palm-tree
    In foreign land, in pleasant place,
    But it would whisper of her face
  And shake its keen sharp blades at me.

" Each black-eyed woman would recall
    A lone church-door, a face, a name,
    A coward's flight, a soldier's shame :
  I fled from woman's face, from all.

" I hugged my gold, my precious gold,
    Within my strong, stout, buckskin vest.
    I wore my bags against my breast
  So close I felt my heart grow cold.

" I did not like to see it now ;
    I did not spend one single piece.
    I travelled, travelled without cease
  As far as Russian ship could plow.

" And when my own scant hoard was gone,
  And I had reached the far North-land,
  I took my two stout bags in hand
As one pursued, and journeyed on.

" Ah, I was weary ! I grew gray ;
  I felt the fast years slip and reel
  As slip black beads when maidens kneel
At altars when out-door is gay.

" At last I fell prone in the road, —
  Fell fainting with my cursèd load.
  A skin-clad cossack helped me bear
  My bags, nor would one shilling share.

" He looked at me with proud disdain, —
  He looked at me as if he knew ;
  His black eyes burned me thro' and thro' ;
His scorn pierced like a deadly pain.

" He frightened me with honesty ;
  He made me feel so small, so base,
  I fled, as if the fiend kept chase, —
The fiend that claims my company !

" I bore my load alone; I crept
    Far up the steep and icy way;
    And there, before a cross there lay
A barefoot priest, who bowed and wept.

" I threw my gold right down and sped
    Straight on.   And oh my heart was light !
    A spring-time bird in spring-time flight
Flies not so happy as I fled.

" I felt somehow this monk would take
    My gold, my load from off my back ;
    Would turn the fiend from off my track,
Would take my gold for sweet Christ's sake !

" I fled ; I did not look behind ;
    I fled, fled with the mountain wind.
    At last, far down the mountain's base
    I found a pleasant resting-place.

" I rested there so long, so well,
    More grateful than all tongues can tell.
    It was such pleasant thing to hear
    That valley's voices calm and clear :

" That valley veiled in mountain air,
    With white goats on the hills at morn ;
    That valley green with seas of corn,
With cottage islands here and there.

" I watched the mountain girls.   The hay
    They mowed was not more sweet than they ;
    They laid brown hands in my white hair ;
They marvelled at my face of care.

" I tried to laugh ; I could but weep.
    I made these peasants one request, —
    That I with them might toil or rest,
And with them sleep the long, last sleep.

" I begged that I might battle there,
    For that fair valley-land, for those
    Who gave me cheer when girt with foes,
And have a country, loved and fair.

" Where is that spot that poets name
    Our country ? name the hallowed land ?
    Where is that spot where man must stand
Or fall when girt with sword and flame ?

"Where is that one permitted spot ?
    Where is the one place man must fight ?
    Where rests the one God-given right
To fight, as ever patriots fought ?

"I say 't is in that holy house
    Where God first set us down on earth :
    Where mother welcomed us at birth,
And bared her breasts, a happy spouse.

"But when some wrong, some deed of shame,
    Shall make that land no more our own —
    Ah ! hunger for that holy name
My country, I have truly known !

"The simple plough-boy from his field
    Looks forth.   He sees God's purple wall
    Encircling him.   High over all
The vast sun wheels his shining shield.

"This King, who makes earth what it is, —
    King David bending to his toil !
    O lord and master of the soil,
How envied in thy loyal bliss !

" Long live the land we loved in youth, —
　　That world with blue skies bent about,
　　Where never entered ugly doubt!
Long live the simple, homely truth!

" Can true hearts love some far snow-land,
　　Some bleak Alaska bought with gold?
　　God's laws are old as love is old;
And Home is something near at hand.

" Yea, change yon river's course; estrange
　　The seven sweet stars; make hate divide
　　The full moon from the flowing tide, —
But this old truth ye cannot change.

" I begged a land as begging bread;
　　I begged of these brave mountaineers
　　To share their sorrows, share their tears;
To weep as they wept, with their dead.

" They did consent.　The mountain town
　　Was mine to love, and valley lands.
That night the barefoot monk came down
　　And laid my two hands in my hands!

"On! On!   And oh the load I bore!
   Why, once I dreamed my soul was lead;
   Dreamed once it was a body dead!
It made my cold, hard bosom sore.

"I dragged that body forth and back —
   O conscience, what a baying hound!
   Nor frozen seas nor frosted ground
Can throw this bloodhound from his track.

"In farthest Russia I lay down
   A dying man, at last to rest;
   I felt such load upon my breast
As seamen feel, who sinking drown.

"That night, all chill and desperate,
   I sprang up, for I could not rest;
   I tore the two bags from my breast,
And dashed them in the burning grate.

"I then crept back into my bed;
   I tried, I begged, I prayed to sleep;
   But those red, restless coins would keep
Slow dropping, dropping, and blood red.

"I heard them clink and clink and clink, —
  They turned, they talked within that grate.
They talked of her; they made me think
  Of one who still must pray and wait.

"And when the bags burned crisp and black,
  Two coins did start, roll to the floor, —
Roll out, roll on, and then roll back,
  As if they needs must journey more.

"Ah, then I knew nor change nor space,
  Nor all the drowning years that rolled
Could hide from me her haunting face,
  Nor still that red-tongued talking gold.

"Again I sprang forth from my bed!
  I shook as in an ague fit;
I clutched that red gold, burning red,
  I clutched, as if to strangle it.

"I clutched it up — you hear me, boy? —
  I clutched it up with joyful tears!
I clutched it close, with such wild joy
  I had not felt for years and years!

"Such joy! for I should now retrace
　　My steps, should see my land, her face;
　　Bring back her gold this battle day,
　　And see her, see her, hear her pray!

"I brought it back — you hear me, boy? —
　　I clutch it, hold it, hold it now:
　　Red gold, bright gold that giveth joy
　　　To all, and anywhere or how;

"That giveth joy to all but me, —
　　To all but me, yet soon to all.
　　It burns my hands, it burns! but she
　　　Shall ope my hands and let it fall.

"For oh I have a willing hand
　　To give these bags of gold; to see
　　Her smile as once she smiled on me
　Here in this pleasant, warm palm-land!"

He ceased, he thrust each hard-clenched fist,
　　He threw his gold hard forth again,
　As one impelled by some mad pain
　　He would not or could not resist.

The creole, scorning, turned away,
  As if he turned from that lost thief, —
  The one that died without belief
That awful crucifixion day.

III.

Believe in man, nor turn away.
  Lo! man advances year by year;
  Time bears him upward, and his sphere
Of life must broaden day by day.

Believe in man with large belief;
  The garnered grain each harvest-time
  Hath promise, roundness, and full prime
For all the empty chaff and sheaf.

Believe in man with proud belief:
  Truth keeps the bottom of her well,
And when the thief peeps down, the thief
  Peeps back at him, perpetual.

Faint not that this or that man fell;
  For one that falls a thousand rise
To lift white Progress to the skies:
  Truth keeps the bottom of her well.

Fear not for man, nor cease to delve
  For cool sweet truth, with large belief.
Lo! Christ himself chose only twelve,
  Yet one of these turned out a thief.

IV.

Down through the dark magnolia leaves
  Where climbs the rose of Cherokee
  Against the orange-blossomed tree,
A loom of moonlight weaves and weaves, —

A loom of moonlight, weaving clothes
  From snow-white rose of Cherokee,
  And bridal blooms of orange-tree,
For fairy folk in fragrant rose.

Down through the mournful myrtle crape,
  Through moving moss, through ghostly gloom,
A long white moonbeam takes a shape
  Above a nameless, lowly tomb;

A long white finger through the gloom
  Of grasses gathered round about, —
  As God's white finger pointing out
A name upon that nameless tomb.

V.

Her white face bowed in her black hair,
  The maiden prays so still within
  That you might hear a falling pin, —
Ay, hear her white unuttered prayer.

The moon has grown disconsolate,
  Has turned her down her walk of stars:
  Why, she is shutting up her bars,
As maidens shut a lover's gate.

The moon has grown disconsolate;
She will no longer watch and wait.

But two men wait; and two men will
Wait on till morning, mute and still:

Still wait and walk among the trees,
　　Quite careless if the moon may keep
　　Her walk along her starry steep
Above the Southern pearl-sown seas.

They know no moon, or set or rise
　　Of stars, or anything to light
The earth or skies, save her dark eyes,
　　This praying, waking, watching night.

They move among the tombs apart,
　　Their eyes turn ever to that door;
They know the worn walks there by heart —
　　They turn and walk them o'er and o'er.

They are not wide, these little walks
　　For dead folk by this crescent town.
　　They lie right close when they lie down,
As if they kept up quiet talks.

VI.

The two men keep their paths apart;
　　But more and more begins to stoop
　　The man with gold, as droop and droop
Tall plants with something at their heart.

Now once again with eager zest
　　He offers gold with silent speech;
　　The other will not walk in reach,
But walks around, as round a pest.

His dark eyes sweep the scene around,
　　His young face drinks the fragrant air,
　　His dark eyes journey everywhere, —
The other's cleave unto the ground.

It is a weary walk for him,
　　For oh he bears a weary load!
　　He does not like that narrow road
Between the dead — it is so dim:

It is so dark, that narrow place,
　　Where graves lie thick, like yellow leaves:

8

Give us the light of Christ and grace,
   Give light to garner in the sheaves.

Give light of love; for gold is cold,
   And gold is cruel as a crime;
   It gives no light at such sad time
As when man's feet wax weak and old.

Ay, gold is heavy, hard, and cold!
   And have I said this thing before?
   Well, I will tell it o'er and o'er,
'T were need be told ten thousand fold.

" Give us this day our daily bread," —
   Get this of God, then all the rest
   Is housed in thine own honest breast,
If you but lift a lordly head.

VII.

Oh, I have seen men, tall and fair,
   Stoop down their manhood with disgust,
   Stoop down God's image to the dust,
To get a load of gold to bear;

Have seen men selling day by day
  The glance of manhood that God gave:
  To sell God's image as a slave
Might sell some little pot of clay!

Behold! here in this green graveyard
  A man with gold enough to fill
  A coffin, as a miller's till;
And yet his path is hard, so hard!

His feet keep sinking in the sand,
  And now so near an opened grave!
  He seems to hear the solemn wave
Of dread oblivion at hand.

The sands, they grumble so, it seems
  As if he walks some shelving brink.
  He tries to stop, he tries to think,
He tries to make believe he dreams:

Why, he is free to leave the land,
  The silver moon is white as dawn;
Why, he has gold in either hand,
  Has silver ways to walk upon.

And who should chide, or bid him stay ?
  Or taunt, or threat, or bid him fly ?
The world's for sale, I hear men say,
  And yet this man has gold to buy.

Buy what ? Buy rest ? He could not rest !
  Buy gentle sleep? He could not sleep,
  Though all these graves were wide and deep
As their wide mouths with the request.

Buy Love, buy faith, buy snow-white truth ?
  Buy moonlight, sunlight, present, past ?
Buy but one brimful cup of youth
  That calm souls drink of to the last ?

O God ! 't is pitiful to see
  This miser so forlorn and old !
O God ! how poor a man may be
  With nothing in this world but gold !

VIII.

The broad magnolia's blooms are white;
  Her blooms are large, as if the moon
Had lost her way some lazy night,
  And lodged here till the afternoon.

Oh, vast white blossoms breathing love!
  White bosom of my lady dead,
  In your white heaven overhead
I look, and learn to look above.

IX.

All night the tall magnolia kept
  Kind watch above the nameless tomb:
  Two shapes kept waiting in the gloom
And gray of morn, where roses wept.

The dew-wet roses wept; their eyes
  All dew, their breath as sweet as prayer.
  And as they wept, the dead down there
Did feel their tears and hear their sighs.

The grass uprose as if afraid
  Some stranger foot might press too near;
  Its every blade was like a spear,
Its every spear a living blade.

The grass above that nameless tomb
  Stood all arrayed, as if afraid
Some weary pilgrim seeking room
  And rest, might lay where she was laid.

X.

'T was morn, and yet it was not morn ;
  'T was morn in heaven, not on earth, —
  A star was singing of a birth,
Just saying that a day was born.

The marsh hard by that bound the lake, —
  The great low sea-lake, Ponchartrain,
  Shut off from sultry Cuban main, —
Drew up its legs, as half awake :

Drew long stork legs, long legs that steep
In slime where alligators creep, —
Drew long green legs that stir the grass,
As when the late lorn night-winds pass.

Then from the marsh came croakings low,
  Then louder croaked some sea-marsh beast;
  Then, far away against the east,
God's rose of morn began to grow.

From out the marsh, against that east,
  A ghostly moss-swept cypress stood ;
  With ragged arms above the wood
It rose, a God-forsaken beast.

It seemed so frightened where it rose !
  The moss-hung thing it seemed to wave
  The worn-out garments of the grave, —
To wave and wave its old grave-clothes.

Close by, a cow rose up and lowed
  From out a palm-thatched milking-shed.
A black boy on the river road
  Fled sudden, as the night had fled :

A nude black boy, a bit of night
  That had been broken off and lost
  From flying night, the time it crossed
The surging river in its flight :

A bit of darkness, following
The sable night on sable wing, —
A bit of darkness stilled with fear,
Because that nameless tomb was near.

Then holy bells came pealing out;
  Then steamboats blew, then horses neighed;
Then smoke from hamlets round about
  Crept out, as if no more afraid.

Then shrill cocks here, and shrill cocks there,
Stretched glossy necks and filled the air.
How many cocks it takes to make
A country morning well awake!

Then many boughs, with many birds, —
  Young boughs in green, old boughs in gray, —
  These birds had very much to say
In their soft, sweet, familiar words.

And all seemed sudden glad; the gloom
Forgot the church, forgot the tomb;
And yet like monks with cross and bead
The myrtles leaned to read and read.

And oh the fragrance of the sod!
  And oh the perfume of the air!
  The sweetness, sweetness everywhere,
That rose like incense up to God!

I like a cow's breath in sweet spring,
  I like the breath of babes new-born ;
A maid's breath is a pleasant thing, —
  But oh the breath of sudden morn !

Of sudden morn, when every pore
  Of mother earth is pulsing fast
With life, and life seems spilling o'er
  With love, with love too sweet to last :

Of sudden morn beneath the sun,
  By God's great river wrapped in gray,
That for a space forgets to run,
  And hides his face as if to pray.

XI.

The black-eyed Creole kept his eyes
  Turned to the door, as eyes might turn
  To see the holy embers burn
Some sin away at sacrifice.

Full dawn! but yet he knew no dawn,
  Nor song of bird, nor bird on wing,
  Nor breath of rose, nor anything
Her fair face lifted not upon.

And yet he taller stood with morn;
  His bright eyes, brighter than before,
  Burned fast against that fastened door,
His proud lips lifting up with scorn, —

With lofty, silent scorn for one
  Who all night long had plead and plead,
  With none to witness but the dead
How he for gold must be undone.

Oh, ye who feed a greed for gold,
  And barter truth, and trade sweet youth
For cold hard gold, behold, behold!
  Behold this man! behold this truth!

Why, what is there in all God's plan
  Of vast creation, high or low,
  By sea or land, by sun or snow,
So mean, so miserly as man?

Lo, earth and heaven all let go
   Their garnered riches, year by year!
The treasures of the trackless snow,
   Ah, hast thou seen how very dear?

The wide earth gives, gives golden grain,
   Gives fruits of gold, gives all, gives all!
   Hold forth your hand, and these shall fall
In your full palm as free as rain.

Yea, earth is generous.   The trees
   Strip nude as birth-time without fear,
   And their reward is year by year
To feel their fulness but increase.

The law of Nature is to give,
   To give, to give! and to rejoice
   In giving with a generous voice,
And so trust God and truly live.

But see this miser at the last, —
   This man who loves, grasps hold of gold,
   Who grasps it with such eager hold,
To hold forever hard and fast:

As if to hold what God lets go ;
    As if to hold, while all around
    Lets go, and drops upon the ground
All things as generous as snow.

Let go your greedy hold, I say !
    Let go your hold !   Do not refuse
    'Till death comes by and shakes you loose,
And sends you shamed upon your way.

What if the sun should keep his gold ?
    The rich moon lock her silver up ?
    What if the gold-clad buttercup
Became a miser, mean and old ?

Ah, me ! the coffins are so true
    In all accounts, the shrouds so thin,
That down there you might sew and sew,
    Nor ever sew one pocket in.

And all that you can hold of lands
    Down there, below the grass, down there,
    Will only be that little share
You hold in your two dust-full hands.

XII.

She comes! she comes! The stony floor
Speaks out! And now the rusty door
At last has just one word this day,
With mute religious lips, to say.

She comes! she comes! And lo, her face
   Is upward, radiant, fair as prayer!
So pure here in this holy place,
   Where holy peace is everywhere.

Her upraised face, her face of light
   And loveliness, from duty done,
   Is like a rising orient sun
That pushes back the brow of night.

How brave, how beautiful is truth!
   Good deeds untold are like to this.
   But fairest of all fair things is
   A pious maiden in her youth:

A pious maiden as she stands
   Just on the threshold of the years
   That throb and pulse with hopes and fears,
And reaches God her helpless hands.

How fair is she !   How fond is she !
　　Her foot upon the threshold there.
Her breath is as a blossomed tree, —
　　This maiden mantled in her hair !

Her hair, her black, abundant hair,
　　Where night, inhabited all night
　　And all this day, will not take flight,
But finds content and houses there.

Her hands are clasped, her two small hands ;
　　They hold the holy book of prayer
　　Just as she steps the threshold there,
Clasped downward where she silent stands.

XIII.

Once more she lifts her lowly face,
　　And slowly lifts her large, dark eyes
　　Of wonder ; and in still surprise
She looks full forward in her place.

She looks full forward on the air
　　Above the tomb, and yet below
　　The fruits of gold, the blooms of snow,
As looking — looking anywhere.

She feels — she knows not what she feels ;
   It is not terror, is not fear,
But there is something that reveals
   A presence that is near and dear.

She does not let her eyes fall down,
   They lift against the far profound :
Against the blue above the town
   Two wide-winged vultures circle round.

Two brown birds swim above the sea, —
Her large eyes swim as dreamily
And follow far, and follow high,
Two circling black specks in the sky.

One forward step, — the closing door
   Creaks out, as frightened or in pain ;
   Her eyes are on the ground again —
Two men are standing close before.

" My love," sighs one, "my life, my all ! "
   Her lifted foot across the sill
   Sinks down, — and all things are so still
You hear the orange blossoms fall.

But fear comes not where duty is,
   And purity is peace and rest;
   Her cross is close upon her breast,
Her two hands clasp hard hold of this.

Her two hands clasp cross, book, and she
Is strong in tranquil purity, —
Ay, strong as Samson when he laid
His two hands forth, and bowed and prayed.

One at her left, one at her right,
   And she between, the steps upon, —
I can but see that Syrian night,
   The women there at early dawn

'T is strange, I know, and may be wrong,
But ever pictured in my song;
And rhyming on, I see the day
They came to roll the stone away.

XIV.

The sky is like an opal sea,
   The air is like the breath of kine,
But oh her face is white, and she
   Leans faint to see a lifted sign, —

To see two hands lift up and wave
  To see a face so white with woe,
  So ghastly, hollow, white as though
It had that moment left the grave.

Her sweet face at that ghostly sign,
  Her fair face in her weight of hair,
  Is like a white dove drowning there, —
A white dove drowned in Tuscan wine.

He tries to stand, to stand erect.
  'T is gold, 't is gold that holds him down !
  And soul and body both must drown, —
Two millstones tied about his neck.

Now once again his piteous face
  Is raised to her face reaching there.
  He prays such piteous, silent prayer
As prays a dying man for grace.

It is not good to see him strain
  To lift his hands, to gasp, to try
  To speak. His parched lips are so dry
Their sight is as a living pain.

I think that rich man down in hell
   Some like this old man with his gold, —
To gasp and gasp perpetual
   Like to this minute I have told.

XV.

At last the miser cries his pain, —
   A shrill, wild cry, as if a grave
   Just ope'd its stony lips and gave
One sentence forth, then closed again.

" 'T was twenty years last night, last night ! "
   His lips still moved, but not to speak ;
   His outstretched hands so trembling weak
Were beggar's hands in sorry plight.

His face upturned to hers, his lips
   Kept talking on, but gave no sound ;
   His feet were cloven to the ground ;
Like iron hooks his finger-tips.

" Ay, twenty years," she sadly sighed :
   " I promised mother every year
   That I would pray for father here,
As she had prayed, the night she died :

" To pray as she prayed, fervidly ;
   As she had promised she would pray
   The sad night of her marriage day,
For him, wherever he might be."

Then she was still ; then sudden she
   Let fall her eyes, and so outspake
   As if her very heart would break,
Her proud lips trembling piteously :

" And whether he come soon or late
   To kneel beside this nameless grave,
May God forgive my father's hate
   As I forgive, as she forgave ! "

He saw the stone ; he understood
   With that quick knowledge that will come
   Most quick when men are made most dumb
With terror that stops still the blood.

And then a blindness slowly fell
   On soul and body ; but his hands
   Held tight his bags, two iron bands,
As if to bear them into hell.

He sank upon the nameless stone
With oh such sad, such piteous moan
As never man might seek to know
From man's most unforgiving foe.

He sighed at last, so long, so deep,
As one heart breaking in one's sleep, —
One long, last, weary, willing sigh,
As if it were a grace to die.

And then his hands, like loosened bands,
  Hung down, hung down on either side;
  His hands hung down and opened wide:
He rested in the orange lands.

University Press: John Wilson & Son, Cambridge.

www.ingramcontent.com/pod-product-compliance
Lightning Source LLC
Chambersburg PA
CBHW020753020726
47495CB00008B/2409